BAD KITTY
Puppy's BIG DAY

NICK BRUEL

A NEAL PORTER BOOK
ROARING BROOK PRESS
New York

For George and Siobhan: friends and family

Copyright © 2015 by Nick Bruel

A Neal Porter Book

Published by Roaring Brook Press

Roaring Brook Press is a division of Holtzbrinck Publishing Holdings Limited Partnership

175 Fifth Avenue, New York, New York 10010

mackids.com

Library of Congress Cataloging-in-Publication Data

Bruel, Nick, author, illustrator.

Bad Kitty : Puppy's Big Day / Nick Bruel. — First edition.

   p. cm

   "A Neal Porter Book."

Summary: Uncle Murray takes Puppy on a walk on a day that Bad Kitty is being unusually difficult, but has several unpleasant encounters with a police officer and one mean dog along the way. Text in interspersed with information about dog behavior, pet care, and more.

   ISBN 978-1-59643-976-4 (hardback)

[1. Dogs—Fiction. 2. Cats—Fiction. 3. Humorous Stories.] I. Title.

   PZ7.B82832Badp 2015

[E]—dc23

2014010357

Roaring Brook Press books may be purchased for business or promotinal use. For information on bulk purchases please contact Macmillan Corporate and Premium Sales Department at (800) 221 7945 x5442 or by email at specialmarkets@macmillan.com

First edition 2015

Printed in the United States of America by

RR Donnelley & Sons Company,

Harrisonburg, Virginia

1   3   5   7   9   10   8   6   4   2

• CONTENTS •

PART ONE
PUPPY LAW 5

PART TWO
PUPPY LOVE 46

PART THREE
PUPPY LOST 72

PART FOUR
PUPPY LOYALTY 138

APPENDIX ONE 154

APPENDIX TWO 155

• PART ONE •

PUPPY LAW

In case it's not obvious, Kitty is in a very, very,

VERY

bad mood today.

And nobody knows why.

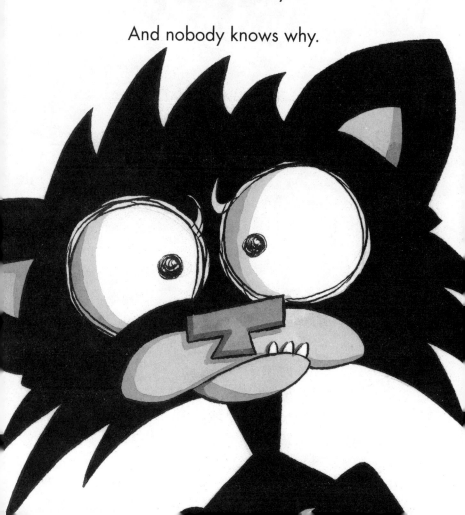

It's worse than the day someone said Kitty needed a bath.

THE DAILY NOOZ
ALL THE NEWS THAT WILL FIT ON PAPER
RAMPAGE

The National Guard was called in yesterday after a local cat refused to take a bath. ...ver seen such ...ntire

It's worse than the day they discontinued her favorite brand of cat litter.

THE DAILY NOOZ
WE MAKE THE NEWS SO YOU DON'T HAVE TO
HORROR

Hundreds fled from a local shopping mall today after a lo...

It's worse than the day they canceled her favorite TV show *Claw and Order*.

THE DAILY NOOZ
MMMM, MMMM . . . NOW THAT'S GOOD NEWS
HORRIBLE RAMPAGE

Hostages were finally released today following a 5-hour stand off that took place after a local cat lost its mind. Police were s—

It's even worse than the day we brought Puppy home.

THE DAILY NOOZ
NEWS, NEWS, IT'S GOOD FOR YOUR HEART. THE MORE YOU READ, THE MORE YOU . . .
RAMPAGING HORROR

What is it with this cat?! Just about every month it has some sort of complete melt— . . . sends every

Speaking of Puppy, here he comes now!

Oh, boy. Puppy, if I were you, I'd leave Kitty alone today. I don't think she's in the mood to play with you. Honestly, I don't think she's EVER in the mood to play with you. But today it'll be like playing with a lit firecracker.

Oh, Puppy. Sometimes you just need to listen to reason.

Too late.

HANG ON, PUPPY! I'M CALLING FOR HELP!

We don't know why Kitty is in such a foul mood. But we really need you to take Puppy out of the house while we either sort this out or move into a new house.

AIEEE

15

WHOA! That was intense! We were lucky to get out of there alive, pooch! Sometimes I'm not convinced she really is a cat. I'm thinking she's more like a weird cross between an electric eel and a howler monkey.

But never mind all that. This ought to be fun! It's been a while since I spent time with a dog. You wanna go to the movies? Or maybe a ball game? Do you know how to play checkers? Maybe we could . . .

19

23

27

Hello again, officer. Lovely day today, isn't it?

YOU GONNA CLEAN UP AFTER THAT DOG?!

Well, officer, do you remember earlier how I was telling you about how I had to leave the house in a big hurry? You remember that, don't you? It was all because of this cat. She can be quite fierce. Really! Anyway, to make a long story short, I left the house so fast that I forgot the leash AND a bag. Silly me! Ordinarily, I would never forget such things. See, I'm quite the advocate of both canine law and sanitation. Why, just the other day my wife was saying to me, "Murray, you should have been a policeman . . .

39

43

KITTY'S HORRIBLE BUT TRUE FACTS ABOUT DOGS

Why Do Dogs Need To Be Walked?

This is poop.

This is a time bomb.

Now imagine if some maniac invented a time bomb filled with poop and pee. Someone did. This monstrous combination is known as a dog.

The only way to diffuse this poop bomb from exploding all over your nice clean home and destroying everything you hold dear is by taking it for a walk.

This is not the case for cats.

Cats are delicate, tidy creatures who perform their elimination under controlled conditions. Meaning, they do their business in a litter box out of view.

But not dogs. Dogs need to be walked at least twice a day so that they can relieve themselves anywhere and everywhere they want regardless of the weather outside. It could be raining baseball bats and you'll STILL have to take that dog outside for the privilege of picking up his droppings with a bag. Lucky you.

This is even worse with puppies who need to pee about every 4 hours. That means you'll be walking him 6 times a day or more unless you want to see your stamp collection float away in a river of urine.

Plus, to make things worse, dogs need those walks for exercise because they don't have the insight to sleep 20 hours a day like cats. Most veterinarians say the average dog should be outside for at least 2 hours a day. Good luck with THAT.

STANDARD DOG-WALKING WEATHER

Let's see now ... You had grilled chicken with herbed garden vegetables dog food this morning. Very nice.

You had garlic roasted beef liver for dinner last night But you didn't like that as much. Understandable. Understandable.

Ah, but you managed to steal some scraps of Chinese food takeout last night as well. Shrimp chow fun, I believe. Clever boy!

Your garden grows tulips in the spring and Russian sage ... no ... sorry, sorry ... Mexican sage in the fall.

You live in a three-bedroom ranch style home with a backyard and a porch and a very ornery cat— sorry about that.

No serious allergies. Your blood pressure is normal. You're due for a distemper booster shot. Your favorite color is yellow. You like sunsets, jazz, and long walks in the park. And you're a Capricorn.

49

So, handsome . . . Now that you and I are boyfriend and girlfriend, I think that you need to give me a lovely little present! Boyfriends always give their girlfriends lovely little presents—beautiful, charming, lovely little presents to express their undying love.

61

67

69

KITTY'S HORRIBLE BUT TRUE FACTS ABOUT DOGS

Why Do Dogs Sniff Butts?

Dogs smell. There are two ways to interpret that sentence. And they're both right.

1. Dogs are smelly. The odor of a wet dog will make you want to rip the nose off your face just to distract you from the pain.

2. Dogs know how to smell. One-third of a dog's brain is dedicated to interpreting smells. (Apparently, the other two-thirds are dedicated to drooling and pooping, but that's a topic for another time.) This means that dogs sense the world around them even more with their noses than they do with their eyes or ears.

A dog's butt gives off a strong odor from an anal gland inside it that can give other dogs a lot of information about it—like what it recently ate, how healthy it is, and even its mood.

So when a dog meets another dog, do they say "Hello. How are you?" No. They can't talk. Do they shake hands? No. They don't have hands. Do they exchange business cards? No. They can't read. Instead, the best way dogs get to know each other is by sniffing each other's butts. Horrible, but true.

Cats, on the other hand, never conduct such behavior. Cats greet each other by licking each other's whiskers, shaking tails, and handing each other formal, handwritten invitations to visit their litter boxes at the earliest convenient opportunity.

Editor's Note: Cats sniff each other's butts, too. They just don't like to talk about it.

Don't you worry, son. You're safe here in the county dog shelter. You get two square meals a day and all the water you can drink. There's a rubber ball around here somewhere to play with, though I ain't seen it in about a year now. And every now and then, an actual beam of sunlight comes through that tiny window up there with the bars. There's nothin' out there in the outside world that can be better than THAT!

Psst. He's crazy.

I should know! I'm **Gramps**! My name is Gramps! But you can call me Gramps. And I've been in here since I was a puppy.

Come to think of it, Gramps is a mighty odd name for a puppy.

But eventually I grew into it. Gramps. I'm Gramps. My name is Gramps.

79

He's old! He's been here too long! He's been institutionalized and doesn't remember what freedom tastes like any more. BUT I DO!

I DO!

Think I'll go find that ball.

Freedom tastes like a hot dog that's rolled off the table and under the sofa and now no one wants it because it's all covered in lint and dust. No one, that is, BUT THE DOG!

Freedom tastes like that delicious slice of ham you snatch up when the baby dips it in applesauce and throws it on the floor because the baby just doesn't appreciate fine cuisine.

Freedom tastes like that big, fat mound of tuna fish that's just sitting there all by itself on the counter, and no one is eating it even though it pleads to you, "Eat me, I beg of you, eat me!" So, the only humane thing to do is to jump up there and eat the tuna fish to put it out of its misery because no one else will do it!

I WANT MY TUNA! I WANT MY HAM! I WANT MY LINT-ENCRUSTED HOT DOG! I WANT MY DELICIOUS, DELICIOUS FREEDOM! AND I SHALL HAVE MY FREEDOM, FOR I AM **HERCULES** AND I HAVE A FOOLPROOF PLAN FOR ESCAPE!

You frighten me.

83

HERCULES' FOOLPROOF

1. COLLECT NAIL CLIPPINGS FROM DOGS.

2. PLACE NAIL CLIPPINGS INTO WAFFLE IRON.

3. REMOVE DELICIOUS LOOKING (BUT PROBABLY INEDIBLE) WAFFLE MADE OUT OF FUSED DOG NAILS.

4. HOLD WAFFLE IN FRONT OF DOGS — CAUSING THEM TO DROOL.

Hey there, young fella! Why so glum? You're young. You're good lookin'. I'd say that you stand a pretty good chance of getting adopted and going home with a nice family.

The rest of us . . . well . . . that's a different story.

Maybe it isn't fair, but folks tend not to adopt the weird ones.

This NEW plan will work! It HAS to. It's even more foolproof than my last plan!

Or the ugly ones—no offense, Miss.

SCRATCH SCRATCH

None taken.

PLAN FOR ESCAPE #592

1) PLACE FUR INTO MACHINE THAT TURNS DOG HAIR INTO CHEESE.

HAIR

CHEESE

PLACE SETTING ON "BRIE"

2) USE CHEESE TO APPLY FEATHERS TO DOGS.

3) FREEDOM!

WOWEE!

I ran away from my owners. They were not very good dog owners. They treated me very badly, so I ran away. I lived in the dog park up until today.

I don't like to talk about it.

Nobody who winds up in here has an owner, Petunia.

That's a fact.

But ... But ... That's not true! I saw him! He was real. He was ...

103

You've got a little microchip just under your skin in the back of your neck that told the shelter who you are and where you live! I bet you didn't even know it was there!

Told ya.

Well, I'll be . . . !

Microchips! Of course! I wish I thought of it!

111

WAITAMINNIT! I'M THAT GUY SHE CHASED AND BIT! BUT I'M NOT PRESSING CHARGES! IT'S OKAY! I'M JUST FINE!

It's not that simple. She may have to go.

BUT I'M . . . wait . . . where do dogs like her "go"?

Well . . .

Hi, dog.

I don't think you like me very much. And you probably trust me even less. But that's because you
don't know me. See, I'm a nice guy. Really. I don't
smoke. I don't gamble. I don't curse . . . well . . .
not that often. I have friends. I have a wife who
loves me. I have a nice car. I have a nice house
with a big backyard. I have a TV with more chan-
nels than I can count. I have a lawn mower. I have
a refrigerator. I have a blender. I have a machine
that can make coffee almost all by itself.

It's kind of incredible, really, when you think about it. All I have to do every morning is pour in a little coffee, pour in a little water, push a button, and five minutes later I have some pretty good coffee. Of course, I have to add in the milk and sugar myself, but . . .

Sorry. I kind of lost track there. What was my point? RIGHT. My point is this—I have lots and lots of stuff. Honestly, I didn't even mention most of the stuff I have.

But the one thing I don't have . . .

C'mon, Gramps! Make with the googly eyes!

I am!

135

KITTY'S HORRIBLE BUT TRUE FACTS ABOUT DOGS | Why Do Dogs Lick Faces?

Cats rarely lick faces, but when they do it's for the same reasons they lick themselves or other cats: to groom you or taste something that might be interesting. Dogs, however, are different. Very different.

GROSS,
DO NOT TOUCH
KEEP AWAY

Dogs lick people because they're hoping to eat any regurgitated food you might have on your face. THAT'S RIGHT! YOU READ THAT RIGHT! DON'T TURN AWAY! FACE THE UGLY TRUTH! Dogs want to eat your throw up!

Say a wild dog, like a wolf mother, kills a deer. Rather than try to drag her prey all the way back to her den, she'll eat as much as she can and then carry her food back inside her stomach. Her puppies will then lick her face to make her regurgitate her food for them to eat. And if this notion doesn't make you want to regurgitate your own breakfast, then I don't know what else will.

This means that when a dog or a puppy licks YOUR face, he's following the same instinct he used when he wanted his mother to vomit on him. I REPEAT . . . Puppies WANT their mothers to vomit on them.

CARTOON BY KITTY

Oh sure, dogs will lick people's faces for other reasons. They like the taste of your salty sweat and tears. They might like the taste of that new skin lotion you're using.

And, of course, dogs like to lick people as a sign of affection or excitement or happiness. Dogs sometimes lick people's faces as a sign of submission just as they once did with their own mothers. Licking is a signal they give to people that they're comfortable around you.

But regardless of the reasons, licking people is gross. Dogs are gross. And licking people is just another item in a long list of disgusting dog habits.

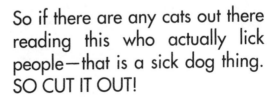

So if there are any cats out there reading this who actually lick people—that is a sick dog thing. SO CUT IT OUT!

*If you LICK, you are SICK!

137

PART FOUR

PUPPY LOYALTY

Okey dokey, pooches! That's done, so let's all go . . .

141

143

WELCOME HOME, PUPPY! Boy, we're glad to have you back safe and sound. But we have to warn you— Kitty is still just as ornery and cross as ever, and we still can't figure out why.

I've been busy digging an underground bunker in the backyard where we can all live from now on.

Puppy, did you hear me? Approaching Kitty right now is probably a terrible idea.

Puppy? Puppy? Uh-oh.

149

Puppy! You found Mousey-mouse! I haven't seen Mousey-mouse since yesterday.

Wait a minute . . .

All this mayhem—all this chaos—all of this wanton carnage and destruction—this is all because Mousey-mouse was missing?

ARE YOU KIDDING ME?!

KITTY, IS THIS WHY YOU'VE BEEN IN SUCH A FOUL, WRETCHED MOOD ALL DAY? IS THIS WHY WE'VE BEEN LIVING IN CONSTANT TERROR ALL THIS TIME? IS THIS WHY THE PIANO IS ON THE ROOF AND THE CAR IS IN THE BASEMENT? IS THIS WHY OUR NEIGHBORS HAVE CHANGED THEIR NAMES AND MOVED OUT OF THE COUNTRY? ALL THIS—ALL THIS BECAUSE YOU COULDN'T FIND MOUSEY-MOUSE FOR ONE STINKING DAY?! IS THIS SOME KIND OF SICK JOKE? KITTY! KITTY! DON'T YOU DARE IGNORE ME. KITTY THIS IS SERIOUS! KITTY, I KNOW YOU CAN HEAR ME! KITTY, WE HAVE TO HAVE A VERY SERIOUS ALL THIS!

MEET THE BREEDS

Petunia • Bulldog
Despite its stern and formidable appearance, the bulldog is a very loving and gentle pet. But they did once have a very savage side to their personality when they were first bred to leap up and bite a bull's nose with their powerful jaws just before bullfights. But this ferocious past is long behind them.

Hercules • Chihuahua
Though considered the smallest dogs in the world and weighing as little as only 2 pounds, chihuahuas can have a fierce and dominating personality. Archaeologists have discovered the remains of these dogs inside of Mayan tombs, because people believed them to be so sacred that they could guide them in the afterlife.

Gramps • Lhasa Apso
The history of these dogs goes back more than 1,300 years to when they were guard dogs in Tibetan monasteries. Though their eyesight is compromised by the long hair that covers their faces, their hearing is exceptionally good. As you can imagine, that luxurious coat of theirs requires daily brushing to stay that way.

Puppy • Mutt
Any dog whose breed cannot be recognized, usually because it's a blend of two or more breeds, is commonly known as a "mutt" or "mongrel." These dogs are just as loving and fun as any purebred. In fact, studies have shown that mutts tend to be healthier and live longer than their purebred cousins.

PET ADOPTION

There are an estimated 6 to 8 MILLION dogs and cats living in pet shelters in the United States. Only about 25 percent of them are ever adopted. Although these shelters do their absolute best to keep their animals healthy and safe, the reality is that they are all overcrowded.

For information on how you can help animals living in shelters go to . . .

humanesociety.org
or
aspca.org

For information on how you can find the right pet for you to adopt from a shelter go to . . .

adoptapet.com
or
petfinder.com

More **BAD KITTY** Madness!

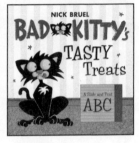

NICK BRUEL is the author and illustrator of the phenomenally successful Bad Kitty series including the 2012 and 2013 CBC Children's Choice Book Award winners *Bad Kitty Meets the Baby* and *Bad Kitty for President*. Nick has also written and illustrated popular picture books including *Who Is Melvin Bubble?* and *Bob and Otto*. Nick lives with his wife and daughter in Westchester, New York. Visit him at nickbruel.com.

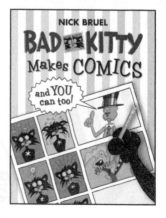

Now that you've read about Bad Kitty, there's more fun to be had with Bad Kitty and her furry friends!

BAD KITTY
Book Club

Dear Kids,

Ask your parents to visit **BadKittyBooks.com** and sign up for the Bad Kitty Kids Club.

Look out for **new** book information, holiday e-cards, fun games and **activities**, special events, sweepstakes, and more.

Thanks and happy reading,

THIS MESSAGE IS BAD KITTY APPROVED